MARC BROWN
Arthur's Science Project

It was Friday. Arthur and his friends were walking home from school.

"Too bad that science project is due Monday," Buster sighed.

"Yeah," Francine agreed.

"Leave it to Mr. Ratburn to spoil our weekend," Muffy added.

At home, Arthur told his dad about the science project.

"I'm making a model of the solar system!" said Arthur.

"Need any help?" asked Dad.

"No, thanks," said Arthur. "I know just what I'm going to do!"

"I've always wanted to make a model of the solar system," said Mom.

She drew a plan for Arthur's project.

"Let's go get supplies at the hardware store," Mom said.

They returned with a large wooden board, pegs, and Styrofoam balls and went to the garage.

"Goggles," said Mom.

"Goggles," Arthur repeated.

"Board...earplugs...drill," Mom called out.

Arthur handed Mom everything she needed.

Arthur watched Mom paint each of the planets.

"Maybe I could help," said Arthur.

"Don't touch that!" cried Mom. "It's not dry!"

"Sorry," said Arthur. "I'll put a second coat on..."

"Doesn't need it," said Mom.

Later Buster, Francine, and Muffy came over to play.

"We're going to the Sugar Bowl," called Buster. "Want to come?"

"We need a break from our projects," said Francine.

"I'm kind of busy," said Arthur.

"Come see Arthur's science project," called Arthur's mom from the house.

"Wow!" said Francine.

"Did you make that yourself, Arthur?" said Buster.

"I better get to work!" sniffed Muffy.

"We all better get to work," said Buster.

Later, Arthur called Buster.

"What am I going to do?" he whispered. "Mom has taken over *my* project..."

"Your project is great!" said Buster. "Can your mom make my model, too?"

"I don't think so," said Arthur.

Arthur hung up the phone and stared into space.

He imagined flying through the galaxy.

"The solar system sure looks different," thought Arthur. "But that astronaut looks very familiar."

"Arthur 2 to Control Center," said Arthur.

"This is Control Center," said Mom. "What's wrong, Arthur 2? Over."

"Everything looks different up here," said Arthur.

"There have been some changes," said Mom. "Some of the planets needed to be painted or replaced."

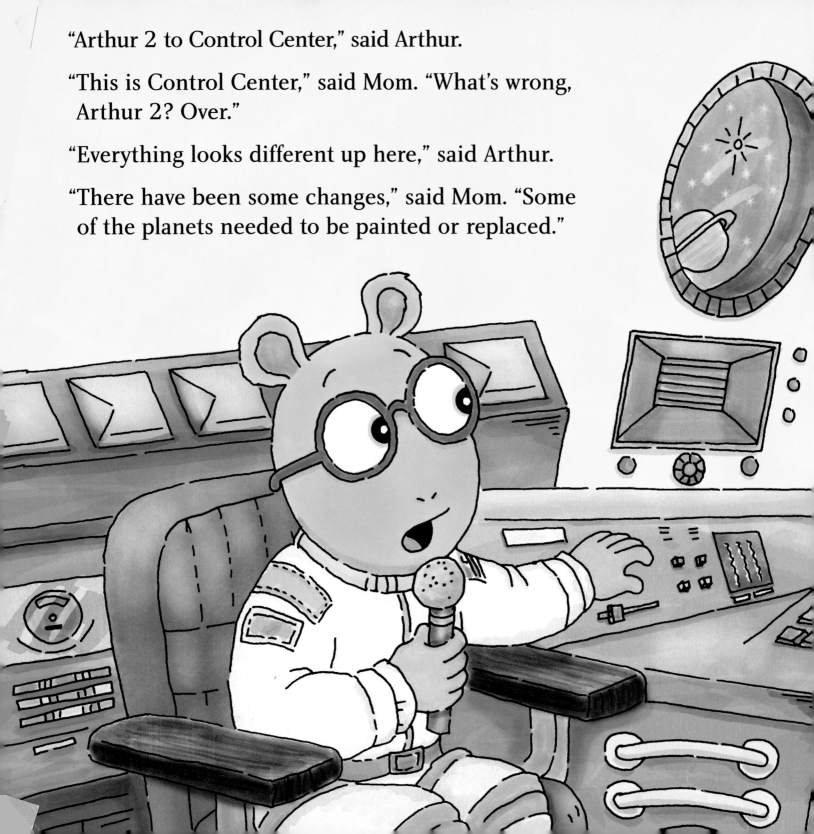

"Arthur 2 to Control Center," said Arthur.

"This is Control Center," said Mom. "What's wrong, Arthur 2? Over."

"Everything looks different up here," said Arthur.

"There have been some changes," said Mom. "Some of the planets needed to be painted or replaced."

Arthur's spaceship stopped at Saturn.

"You missed a spot on the ring!" he called.

"Thanks!" said Mom. "I'm done! What do you think?"

"It's very bright," said Arthur. "I would have picked different colors."

"Earth to Arthur!" said D.W.

Arthur shook his head.

"Are you all right?" asked Mom.

"Fine," said Arthur. "I just have a lot to do!"

He ran up to his room.

Later, Arthur came downstairs carrying a mobile.

"You made your own solar system," said Mom.

"I hope you don't mind," said Arthur.

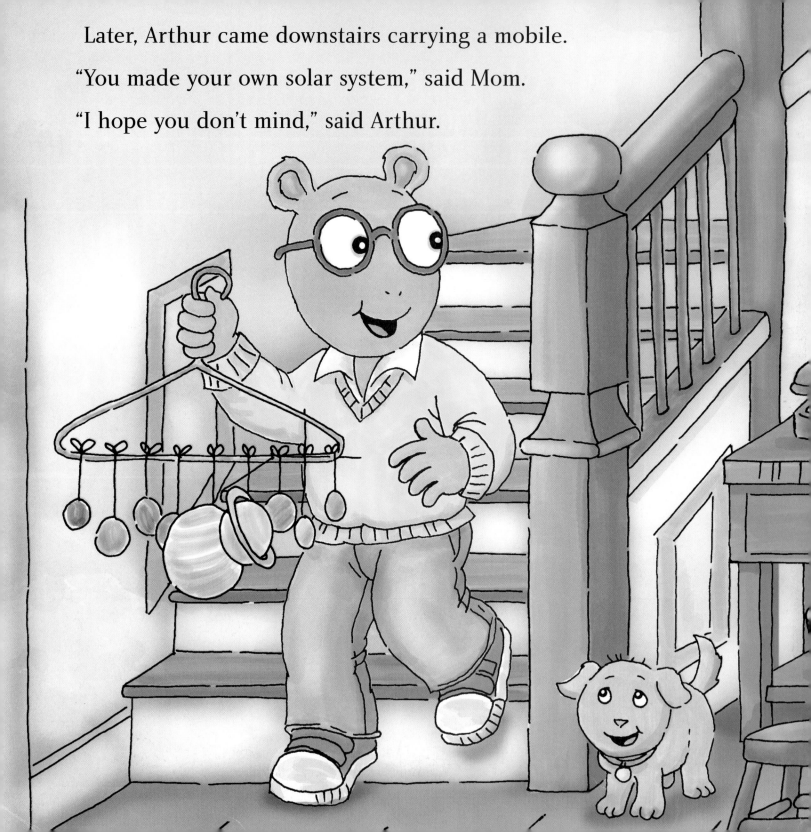

"It's great!" said Mom. "I guess I got a little carried away."

"Just a little," said Arthur.

"I've got an idea," said Arthur. "Put your name on your project, and I'll turn them both in. Maybe Mr. Ratburn will give us extra credit."